Cambridge Early Years

Mathematics

Learner's Book 2C

Alison Borthwick & Cherri Moseley

Contents

Note to parents and practitioners — 3

Block 5: Growing — 4

Block 6: Animals — 18

Acknowledgements — 32

Note to parents and practitioners

This Learner's Book provides activities to support the third term of Mathematics for Cambridge Early Years 2.

Activities can be used at school or at home. Children will need support from an adult. Additional guidance about activities can be found in the **For practitioners** boxes.

Children will encounter the following characters within this book. You could ask children to point to the characters when they see them on the pages, and say their names.

The Learner's Book activities support the Teaching Resource activities. The Teaching Resource provides step-by-step coverage of the Cambridge Early Years curriculum and guidance on how the Learner's Book activities develop the curriculum learning statements.

Hi, my name is Mia.

Find us on the front covers doing lots of fun activities.

Hi, my name is Gemi.

Hi, my name is Rafi.

Hi, my name is Kiho.

Block 5 Growing

What's the same?

Find, circle and say.

Talk about the object that is similar to the shape at the beginning of the row.

 sphere

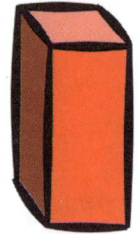 cuboid

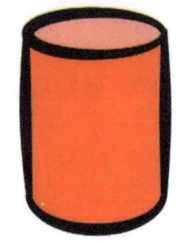 cylinder

 cube

For practitioners

Encourage children to describe the characteristics of the named shape, then look along the row to find an object with the same characteristics. Challenge children to say what is different about the other two objects.

Cuboids and cylinders

Match and say.

Compare each object to the cylinder and cuboid. Which one is a good match?

For practitioners

Encourage children to describe the characteristics of one of the shapes in the middle, then find the objects with the same characteristics. Ask questions such as *Why have you matched that to the cylinder and not the cuboid?* Challenge children to talk about how it is similar to the shape as well as how it is different.

Cubes and spheres

Match and say.

Compare each object to the cube and sphere. Which one is a good match?

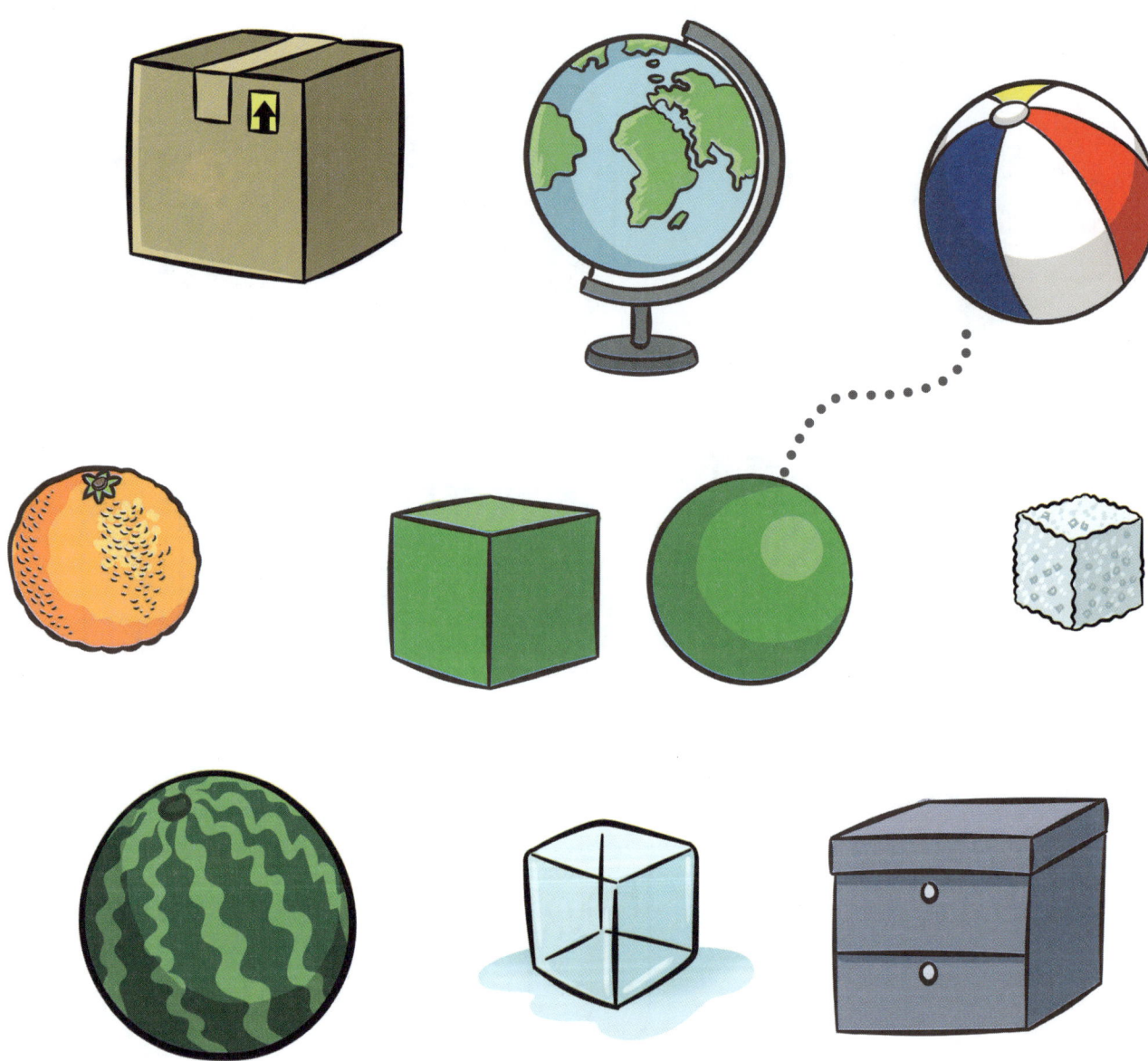

For practitioners
Encourage children to describe the characteristics of one of the shapes in the middle, then find the objects with the same characteristics. Ask questions such as *Why have you matched that to the sphere and not the cube?* Challenge children to suggest other cubic or spherical objects.

Different shapes

Find, circle and say.

> Compare each object to the named shape.

 sphere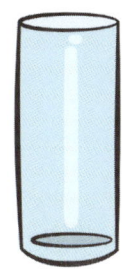

 cuboid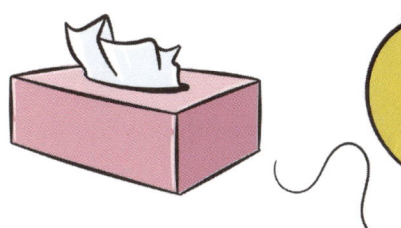

 cylinder

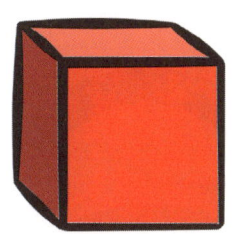 cube

For practitioners
Encourage children to describe the characteristics of the named shape, then look along the row to find the object that is different. Challenge children to talk about how it is similar to the shape as well as how it is different.

Shape match

Match and say.

Compare each object to the triangle, rectangle, square and circle. Which one is a good match?

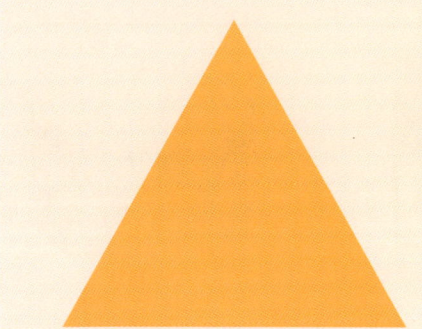 

For practitioners
Encourage children to describe the characteristics of one of the four shapes in the middle, then look at the objects to find those with the same characteristics. Ask questions such as *Why have you matched that to the square?* Invite children to suggest other objects to match the shapes.

More shapes around us

Colour and say.

Colour all the circles ◯ yellow.
Colour all the triangles △ red.
Colour all the squares ☐ purple.
Colour all the rectangles ▭ blue.

Colour the shape in the instructions, then colour all the matching shapes in the picture the same colour.

For practitioners

Encourage children to describe the characteristics of each named shape, then look at the picture to find and colour all the matching shapes. Ask children where they have seen a circle, triangle, square or rectangle.

Which one doesn't belong?

Circle and say.

Think about the shape of each object, not what it is.

  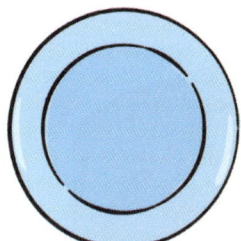

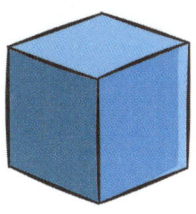 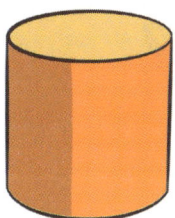 

 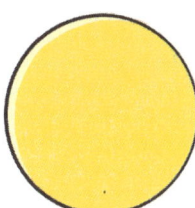 

For practitioners

Encourage children to tell you why their chosen shape does not belong. If children choose one that does not belong based on reasons other than shape, remind them to look at the shape of the objects. There are no wrong answers, provided children can give a reason for their choice. Invite children to think of other objects that are the same shape as the shape that does not belong.

Animal match
Match and say.

Find 2 animals with tails, or with the same number of legs, or wings, or something else.

For practitioners
Encourage children to identify the characteristics of an animal, then look at the other animals to see if they also have one of the characteristics. Challenge children to find a pair of animals that they can join together twice, for two different reasons. Ask *What is different about those two animals?*

Yellow class

Sort and write.

Are there more children who are 4 than children who are 5?

First find all the children who are 4 and count them.

_____ children are 4.   _____ children are 5.

There are more children who are _____

than children who are _____ .

For practitioners
Some children will find it helpful to use coloured cubes. They could put a cube of one colour on each child wearing a '4' badge and a cube of another colour on each child wearing a '5' badge. They can then use one-to-one correspondence to compare the two groups of cubes and answer the question.

Buttons

Count and write.

Are there more buttons with 2 holes or 4 holes?

There are more

For practitioners

Encourage children to first mark (by ticking, circling or crossing out) either all the buttons with 2 holes or 4 holes, counting as they find them, then use a different mark to count the other set of buttons. Tell them to then compare the numbers. Challenge children to ask another question about the buttons and answer it.

Yellow class's shoes

Compare and draw.

Which type of shoe do most children in this class wear?

Most children wear

The fewest children wear

For practitioners

Read the question to the children. Encourage children to use the graph to complete the boxes. Challenge children to ask and answer other questions such as *Are there fewer superhero shoes than boots? How do you know? How many more sandals are there than trainers? How could you check?*

Which objects are missing?

Find and tick.

Draw the missing objects in the correct party bag.

For each bag, tick each object in the table. If there is no tick, that object is missing.

1

2

3

4

Object		Party bag 1	Party bag 2	Party Bag 3	Party bag 4
Ball		✔	✔	✔	✔
Elephant					
Lollipop					
Smiley face sticker					
Dinosaur					
Sweet					
Pencil					

For practitioners

Encourage children by asking questions such as *Have all the party bags got a ball? They are all ticked in the table. What shall we check next?* Invite children to draw another party bag – will it have one or more objects missing?

Block 6 Animals

Which one is longer?
Circle.

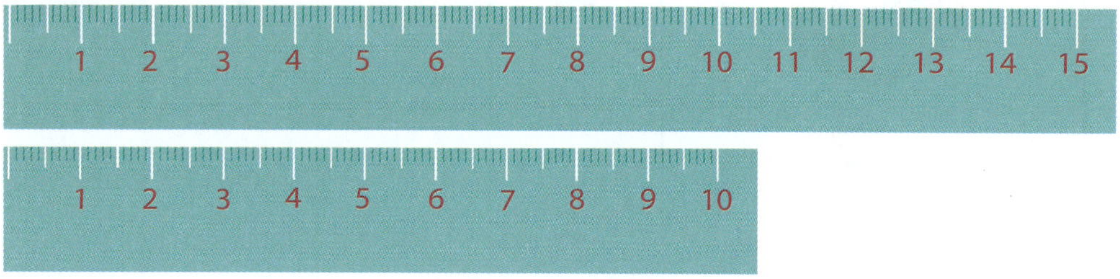

Check that the objects are lined up at one end and then look at the other end to see which object is longer in each pair.

For practitioners
Children circle the longer item of each pair. Ask *How do you know this pencil is longer than this one?* Invite children to look around their environment and find two objects where one is longer than the other.

Comparing lengths
Tick and say.

Try drawing a line to help you compare the objects.

Which is longer?

Which is shorter?

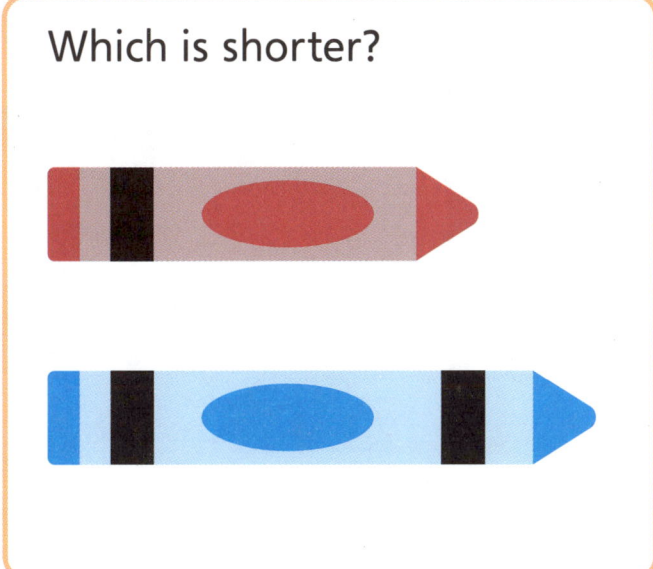

Which is taller?

Which is shorter?

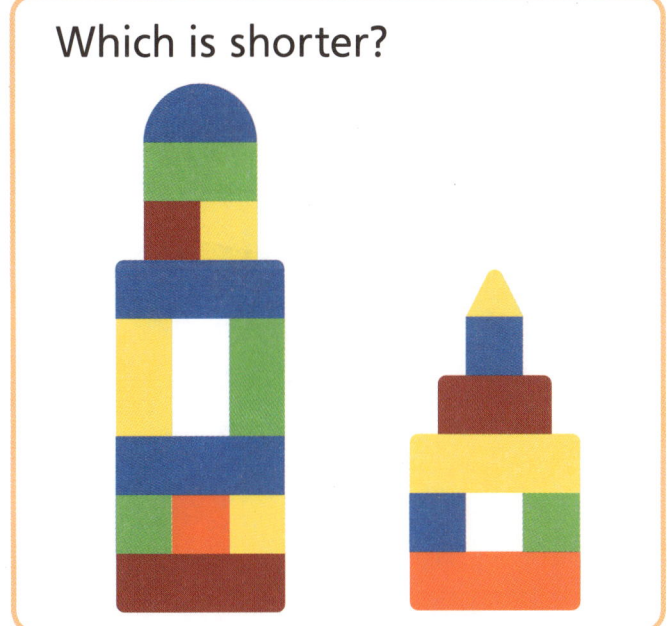

For practitioners
Ask children to explain why they have ticked a particular object. Ask *How do you know this object is shorter than this one?* Challenge children to look around their environment and find two objects where one object is shorter than the other.

Which is heavier?
Tick and say.

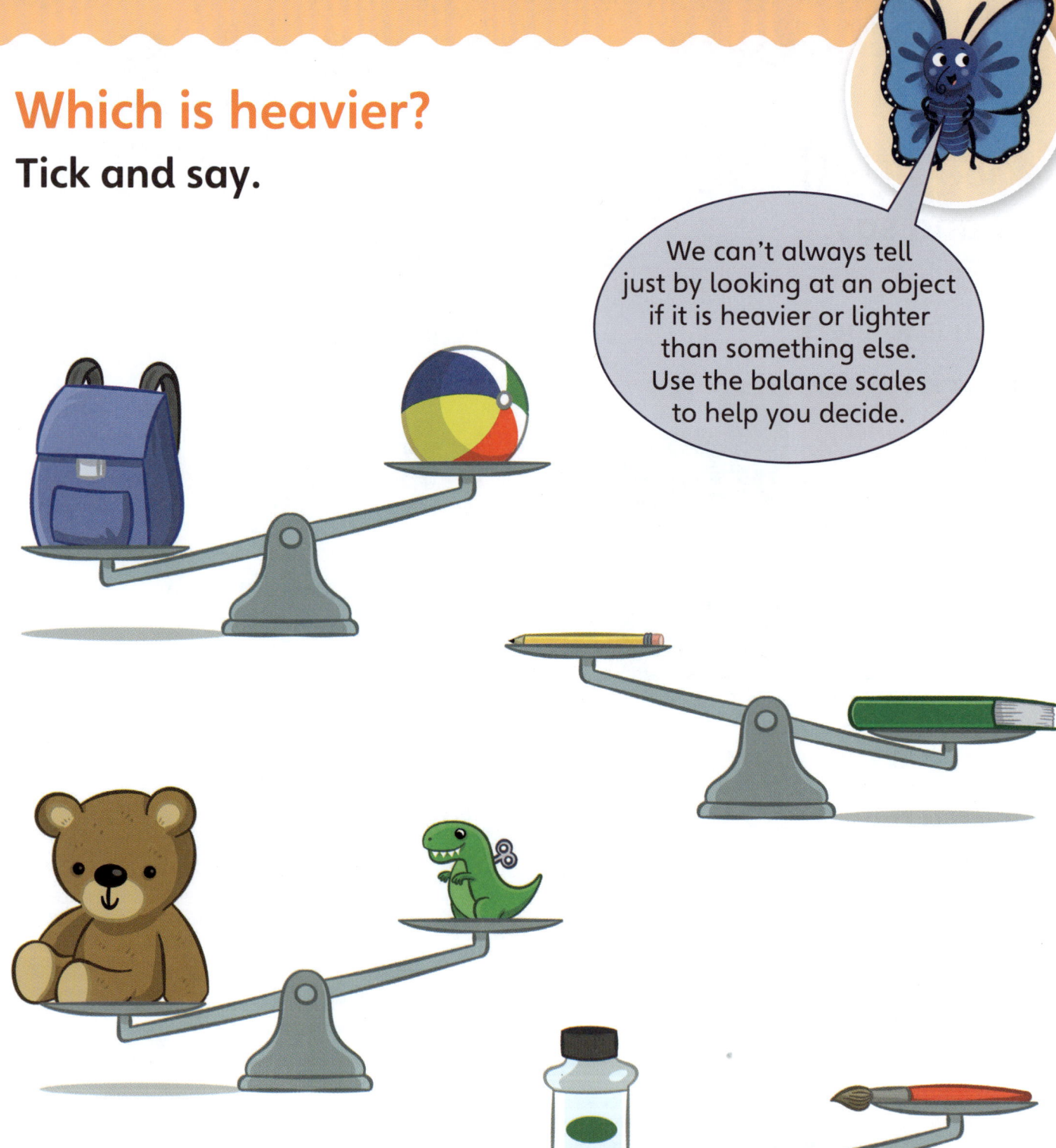

We can't always tell just by looking at an object if it is heavier or lighter than something else. Use the balance scales to help you decide.

For practitioners
Challenge children to explain how they know which object is heavier in each pair.

Surprise!

Circle.

Hari compared the masses of some objects.
He was surprised by one of the results.
Circle the result you think he is surprised by.

For practitioners

Encourage children to look at each picture and say whether they think that one might have surprised Hari. If necessary, point out that Hari may have been surprised that the balloon is much bigger in size than the pebble but the balloon is lighter. Challenge children to suggest other pairs of objects that might also cause a surprise when their masses are compared.

Which box does each animal fit into?
Match.

Try to imagine the toy animal fitting inside the box.

For practitioners
Invite children to look at each toy animal and decide which box it might fit into. Remind children that all the animals need to match to a box. Ask children to see if objects from the setting fit inside containers. Ask *Will these pencils fit inside this box? How do you know?*

Which container holds more?

Circle.

Circle the container that holds more in each pair.

Remember, we can't always tell just by looking whether a container holds more or less than another container.

For practitioners

Ask children to look at the two containers in each set and circle which container holds more than the other. Discuss the bottom right pair, talking about how they know which container holds more.

Double the objects

Draw and write.

Draw objects to show double.
Write the total.

Can you say how many without counting?

Double 4 is ____ .

Double 1 is ____ .

Double 3 is ____ .

For practitioners
Encourage children to count the objects if they cannot say how many without counting. They can touch each picture as they count it.

Double spots

Colour and write.

Colour the same number of spots on each five frame to show double the number.

Try putting counters on each five frame first and then colour where you put each counter.

Double 2 is ____.

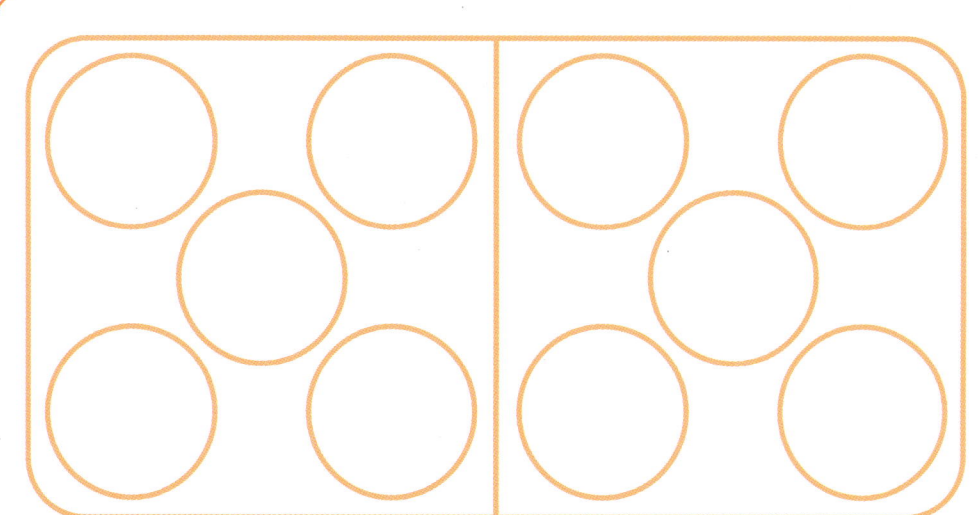

Double 4 is ____.

For practitioners

Encourage children to colour 2 spots on one five frame and then 2 spots on the other five frame to show double 2. Ask *What do you notice? What does double mean?* Invite children to spot doubles around the setting.

Dice doubles

Draw and write.

Draw the same number of spots on each dice to show double the number.

> Look at each pair of dice. Do both dice look the same?

Double 1 is ____ .

Double 3 is ____ .

Double 5 is ____ .

For practitioners

If available, give children two real dice to look at. Invite children to draw spots on one of the dice pictures first and then draw the corresponding number of spots on the other dice. Invite children to think about and explain what double 0 means.

Share the honey equally
Match.

Try it out with teddy bears and objects first.

For practitioners
Talk to children about what sharing equally means. Challenge children to offer a solution when they cannot share the jars equally. Ask *What could we do? How might we solve this problem?*

Share the apples equally
Draw.

Share 8 apples.

Share 8 apples.

For practitioners
Give children objects (such as counters and small world people) so they can try the activity practically first. Challenge children to fairly share other amounts between 2 or 4 people, including an odd number of objects.

What happens when there are more children?

Halves or not halves?

Tick and cross.

Tick ✔ the shapes that are divided into halves. Cross ✘ the shapes that are not divided into halves.

Finding half means dividing the shape into two equal parts. Each part is a half.

For practitioners
Invite children to look at each shape and decide if it is divided into halves. Ask *How do you know?* Challenge children to draw fun shapes that are divided into halves and not halves.

Quarters

Tick and cross.

Tick ✔ the shapes that are divided into quarters. Cross ✘ the shapes that are not divided into quarters.

Finding a quarter means dividing the shape into four equal parts. Each part is a quarter.

For practitioners

Invite children to look at each shape and decide if it is divided into a quarters. Ask *How do you know?* Challenge children to draw fun shapes that are divided into quarters and not quarters.

Who has more?

Circle.

There is the same food at each party. Which children would get more? Why?

The more children there are, the less each child gets.

Party 1

Party 2

For practitioners

Invite children to say what they can see. Ask *How many sandwiches would each child get at Party 1? How many sandwiches would each child get at Party 2? Why? Which party would you prefer to go to? Why?* Challenge children to create a party role-play and explore sharing items between different groups of toys.

Acknowledgements

The authors and publishers acknowledge the following sources of copyright material and are grateful for the permissions granted. While every effort has been made, it has not always been possible to identify the sources of all the material used, or to trace all copyright holders. If any omissions are brought to our notice, we will be happy to include the appropriate acknowledgements on reprinting.

Thanks to the following artists at Beehive Illustration:

Lays Bittencourt, Tamara Joubert, John Lund, Michelle McGovern, Sarah Pitt, Conor Rawson, Joe Wilkins.

Cover characters by Becky Davies (The Bright Agency)